2027

The revelation

Juan Manuel Rodríguez Caamaño

2027
The revelation
Juan Manuel Rodríguez Caamaño

First edition November 2019
First published Mexico City, November 2019

Registration number: 03- 2019- 090910550300- 01

"I could not dedicate this work to anyone other than the one who has always accompanied me in my life, in any project, on any green or winding road, dedicated this novel to God because he has given me inspiration in each of the wonders of the nature."

2027

The revelation

Juan Manuel Rodríguez Caamaño.

May 27, 2027, El Paso, Texas.

Hi, I'm Robert Anstead, crewman of the missing Pioneer 17 spacecraft, designed to travel to Jupiter. Probably nobody will believe the adventure that I lived in unknown and unimaginable places.

Surely, when they finish reading my testimony, two things will happen: they will think that I am crazy or that I suffer from schizophrenia, because the described beings can only be taken out of the imagination; and it will be incredible to discover who led me to live this unforgettable and terrifying story, and how I returned to Earth. In both scenarios there is no logic and they will say that it is unreal.

The adventure began on February 23, 2027, with the launch of Pioneer Mission 17, designed to conquer Mars. We had already won the war by first arriving at the Moon, and at NASA, Mars was better known than Africa.

Launching a risky mission to Jupiter, for the United States it was morally necessary to conclude the decade by reaffirming space and military supremacy, after the controversy of being the first to step on the Moon, and after making some expeditions to Mars; We felt obliged to explore challenging horizons, applying the technology of our laboratories and the experience acquired, confirming who the dominant power was. Decades of investing billions of dollars in NASA, they ruled the institution to make quick decisions due to the strong pressure of Congress, dominated in recent years by a socialist ideology. Lawmakers questioned: - Why invest so much money in something that did not represent a palpable benefit to the country? - Invariably, the question caused more stress than any extra-terrestrial threat.

Neither my classmates nor I could refuse the expedition; Nationalism was our only reason for being, so the word "no" was suppressed when it came to raising the flag of stars and stripes somewhere in the universe.

I can assume, without fear of being mistaken, that those who see this testimonial recording will doubt that it is Robert Anstead, or they will think that I made it before the trip, because for my country I am dead, or at least they told me at the time they lost contact with my crew. Perhaps, because of the incredible story I will tell, they will want to put me in a psychiatric hospital, or worse, they will seek my death.

Day 0. The event.

The take-off was successful; while our ship was propelled and slowly moved away from the planet, an indescribable sensation invaded me: before my eyes the Earth was reduced, being something immense and infinite, it became, second to second, something finite and tiny. I was no longer one in a million, I was one of three crew members among ten billion inhabitants.

The best thing about space travel was that compared to the videos we watched for almost a decade about the arduous preparation of previous crews, the dehydrated food that had to be ingested did not taste so unpleasant. While the ship was moving away there was no sign that it could crash. I still remember that John Barnes, - my companion of so many adventures -, and I, played on the metal chess board, designed for less gravity, perhaps for that reason, the moment of the accident happened unnoticed.

From the window of the Pioneer 17, I was dazzled by the atmosphere and the sun's rays on Earth ... to my mind came the glorious moment in which my name would appear in the annals of history like Armstrong and Aldrin, the first to step on the Moon. As a child my goal was to travel to space, I always loved science, applied in classes, looking for the opportunity, begged my parents to take me to the places where they exposed great inventions and there were games in which the boys had fun and learned Physics, Chemistry or Astronomy.

Being immortal was a latent idea ...After the mission that seemed to take place at that time, there were sacrifices, decades of much study, where analysing the universe was my passion; an impeccable physical preparation in which, the main part was to be willing to risk life on the first manned visit to Jupiter, I travelled with the highest risk of all expeditions in the history of NASA.

Jupiter is further from the Sun than Mars, therefore, it must have extremely cold weather conditions; so much that the three passengers gave us the chills to think of some failure in our space suits with which we would descend. However, at NASA nothing failed, everything was perfect.

The flag that we would raise had been made with some alloys and carbon mixtures to prevent the three colors from being erased despite the extreme weather. I remember reading complete books that talked about how the decision was made about who should take the first step on the moon on July 20, 1969, there were many criteria that were considered. At first it was Aldrin who would have the honor, and in the end, after an analysis of the crew's career, they chose Armstrong.

My two companions and I discussed that on Earth for many days and hours drinking cold German beer, both in the last summer and winter, also planning the return to each of our native villages being world heroes.

John Barnes was from Minnesota, maybe that's why the cold didn't scare him as much as it did us; Joseph Collins and I were descendants of Mexicans, we came from two border locations that once belonged to Mexico: John of Anaheim, California; and me from Mission, Texas. Sometimes the three of us fantasized about the moment when we would descend on American soil and then when we arrived at our cities and see crowds cheering.

The best of living together, in the little free time we took advantage of in any bar near our residence, was the plan we put together. No one knew him, not even NASA, and we would do it in Jupiter. Once the hatch of the Pioneer 17 was closed and in orbit, we would decide, in a chess tournament, who would go out first, but that would only be the order to leave the ship since the first would wait for the second and the third, then we would take of the shoulders on the ledge and

thus embraced we would take the first step in Jupiter. - Why didn't Armstrong and Aldrin do it this way? -That enormous passion of the Americans and in general of the human being for the competition, where there is a winner and many defeated, also creates a sense of selfishness and disunity. Well they could step on the Moon at the same time as we thought we would do in Jupiter, but no, the order was to show that, that only one had to dominate: he won USA, won Armstrong and closed case.

We wanted a message against individualism, a blunt blow; that there is nothing stronger than united wills and shared merit. That united us more, we were like three inseparable brothers looking to take their country to the top, as if it were a joint sport with all the difficulties that this entails. The last few years were not only of exhaustive preparation but also of living almost twenty-four hours a day with them: we ate breakfast, ate, ate, drank and practiced hard, always together.... Everything happened when I was facing the imposing landscape of the Earth, changing in size and tones, motivated by being part of the story and excited to be about to win a game of chess to John, a triumph I would pay to be the first to leave from the hatch reaching Jupiter. My queen had just four vertical frames, just by moving the pawn and facing her king, I would give her checkmate. I did so, with my left hand I raised the queen in slow motion to put it with extreme firmness on the board and uttered the words "checkmate" but instantly everything went dark.

It is the last thing I remember about the expedition, as if someone had pressed the shutdown button; in fractions of a second I felt an intense cold that was entering through the skin until the bones were penetrated and the last conscious neuron, at which time I lost consciousness. For a moment I thought about the improbable theory of a failure in the ship, honestly, I never completely trusted technology, I knew that in any machine there is a probability of

error, so it happened after orbiting the universe in search of new and urgent sources of energy before the shortage on Earth, but the strong impact of cold emitted for unknown reasons could not be due to a slowdown of the ship, because I did not appreciate any movement or shock. Everything went out, as if my head was disconnected.

Day 1. Somewhere.

When I opened my eyes, everything lit up, as if my pupils illuminated the darkness, they worked with a type of sensor activated to the movement of the eyelids, -I remembered the motion sensors that are programmed in the buildings to save energy- and also attracted my hatred to these devices because on more than one occasion I ran out of light while I was in the bathroom, having to use the cell phone lamp, something unpleasant and complicated.

I didn't know what time of day it was; neither could I calculate it with the sun's brightness because the lighting hue did not resemble that of the king star, or any other type of artificial light known. Then I auscultated my body to confirm that I didn't have any injuries. The traveling suit I was wearing was intact and still retained the first thin layers; the thickest part and where there were some controls on the ship, they were gone. I realized that I was lying on an extensive and comfortable bed of an unknown material, softer than silk and padded in a way that generated satisfaction to my muscles.

When I got up, the bed was automatically picked up from the bottom to give me more space in what looked like the empty room of a luxury hotel. Everything was of an extremely intense white, something that my eyes had not experienced before, could not distinguish the source of light, it seemed that the sun emitted luminescence that penetrated every corner. For a moment I thought that after the space accident we had returned to Earth and were under observation; as in quarantine.

At first glance there was no more furniture than the bed. Suddenly, on the right side, a flat surface began to descend from the wall, like a silver metallic table, which was previously camouflaged; I deduced that it was a table when I discovered some known fruits, but of a strange size, with a more square shape than usual, for example, the manila mango, like the one harvested on my father's ranch and that both we like to eat in May and June, it was of an impressive size, its size resembled that of a papaya or fruit pump as the Cubans call it; I immediately began to taste it, not knowing if it was mine or if it could be a trap; with the first bite I forgot any worries, it was the sweetest fruit I had tasted. I was stunned because when I ingested it, a kind of nutritional table was projected on the wall and the table; on the first bite a number appeared and each bite was added, I could not believe that each bit of food ingested was counted on the screen!

The same happened when I tried a piece of baked tuna, at first it was not to my liking, since I was not used to eating it, but finally I succumbed to the taste.

Looking for answers, I began to walk the corners of the room with my hand; I had barely advanced a couple of meters, when an alarm, with a slight sound, began to sound and on the nutritional board, a red light indicated that I should finish the food, apparently, they were part of a diet perfectly designed by experts and should abide by the directions on the strange board. When I felt like going to the bathroom, a small space formed in one of the corners of the room where I indicated with drawings where to do it. I was a few seconds of urinating anywhere because I could not find where and had ingested almost a liter of what looked like water, but this liquid was thicker.

Until that time, no window was observed.

Day 2. The imperceptible window.

It looked like a whitish wall over the rectangular and immense room, according to my calculations it was about five or six meters long and about three and a half high; suddenly, inexplicably, the space was taking shape, first, as a painting in the process of creation, then that of a television with a white screen off in which, when turned on, the image gradually became sharper, until it seemed a high resolution photograph and become something very similar to a window to the outside.

The room was in the center of a large place with intense and dazzling greenery vegetation; and both were part of a scenario of several ascending levels, like a small colosseum built with a marble-like material. At first, I laughed imagining that perhaps it was not a window but a giant screen the size of a wall, the largest.

In it I saw, but was also observed by funny characters, similar to those in the movie "Star Wars," thin, hairy, large, tiny, long, with limbs of all kinds of shapes and textures; they were staring at my face and it seemed they were commenting on me, it was then one of them threw a small, jelly-like object from what resembled a mouth.

When I saw the semi-liquid dripping on the wall, I realized that it was not a screen but a window; my body shuddered, and I was terrified by the presence of the horrible characters surrounding my cell and with unknown intentions. Then I tried to calm down, thinking that perhaps the window was like those of police interrogations, where it can only be seen outside and not inside.

Confident in my theory, I continued searching to not think about the unknown beings; I touched all the walls to detect some other hidden mechanism that could allow me to access another place or free myself.

But it was useless, it seemed that everything I had seen work was executed by someone outside. So, there was nothing left but to continue observing the gigantic window, where the presence of strange beings was added, such as the large animal with very long claws covering the entire space. Fear invaded me, since the entities that were approaching looked unpleasant and fierce; there was one, the most grotesque, with strange movements that inspired terror, especially when from the lower part of his huge body appeared something long, pointed from where a black and viscous liquid drained, like the oil of the car, when it came so close to me , made contact with the window and the blow rumbled like a huge hammer, but did not dent the glass that protected me, I only felt terror and raised the adrenaline.

Fortunately, the glass was only beaten, however, in an instant, as if it had an automatic windshield, it was cleaned and dried, so it seemed that the wall could absorb or aspirate any substance. I didn't understand anything, if uncertainty terrified me, situations like that stressed me out more.

Many images passed through my head, I remembered the traumatizing moment when we were traveling and everything got dark; I feared for my companions, I didn't know his whereabouts, and to top it off, I didn't know where he was. My family worried me, they were surely worried, desolate, being the eldest of their children, their first adoration and their greatest pride, especially when they knew that they would participate in a historical space mission.

I wanted to go home and drink a cup of coffee by the fireplace, do the morning routine with my parents, laughing always, being treated like a true king and with my hairy dog, beautiful and playful.

My God, how much I wanted to know where I was. I felt with a tiny being, cornered, dominated, without will, like a puppet, terrified, so I couldn't stand it anymore and threw myself on the floor to cry in rage and helplessness. Suddenly, a slight but latent sound seemed to give instructions in different types of languages, even some were sounds without words, others seemed like Morse code, but with a longer space.

I remembered the first time at the zoo with my father.

Day 3. Discovering the place.

I began to explore every hidden space in the room looking for answers; I tried to take the unfortunate situation very calmly, because something was certain, my dream of stepping on Jupiter was diluted.

I remembered when I was a teenager and addicted to video games, I spent hours trying to find the secrets in every inch of the screen. Now it was not one of those, it was my integrity that was exposed, that was in the anxiety, and had only one chance, not as in games where I had several lives to continue the mission, here there was only one and I was afraid to risk it.

I looked slowly at every millimeter of the wall at what other options there were, apart from the ones I had discovered; I already knew how to unfold the bed, request food and access the bathroom, that's how in the counter corner of the toilet I found something that seemed to be a computer, a screen where I could write and process mathematical data. On the electronic board I wrote down details that I remembered from the moment before the alleged collision: coordinates, temperature inside and outside the ship, distance to reach Jupiter, speed, quantity of supplies, available fuel, oxygen of each of the crew, energy consumed and available to return home.

I highlighted the tasks to be carried out reaching the objective, including raising the flag, taking samples of the soil in different parts of the planet and photos of all the explored places; place several sensors on the Jupiterian surface to get us information about the multiple orographic variables, which would allow us to understand the behavior of the meteorological phenomena of that planet, as well as the characteristics of the existing soil and minerals.

Finally, I recorded the pressure of the ship, the altitude at which we would be and the objects that could hinder the expedition.

Sometimes, when traveling by plane, I was aware of the fact that I was in the air, miles high, in a cabin the size of a room; but when I climbed into Pioneer 17, that feeling became even more exciting, since the space was narrow, and I was immersed and helpless in outer space, seeing the tiny Earth.

Eureka! I still remembered all the data of the space travel, now I could feel calm, at least, somewhere the information of the mission to Jupiter would be stored, although in the circumstances in which I was, the fact of writing had only served to decrease the Anguish, perhaps, nothing I wrote would remain saved.

I finished capturing the information and continued to feel the walls trying to find new digital options to activate some other service. I found the basics: turn on the lights, close the huge window at night to rest, play music of my liking, more options to rest, such as quite comfortable furniture and something similar to a hammock; I could see all kinds of images of the place; the vegetation was vast and the flowers had intense colors. I also discovered that there was no human way to escape or any visible option.

I assumed that whoever was my captor, tried to make me healthy and happy, that within total uncertainty, was comforting. However, I was also worried, remember that, in the ranches, the cattle are fed and cared for to sacrifice it as part of the food chain, I could not have communication with the Earth, - I did not even want to become the food of another species!

Day 4. That strange company.

I woke up crying, remembering how much I hated zoos, since childhood I was irritated to see animals treated as slaves, locked only to serve as an ornament and joy to visitors. It was annoying to see the little ones throwing any object at the helpless specimens. But what caused me the most despair was to think that because of the confinement, they felt limited, without running freely, without will, destined to die behind bars.

And if the cloister of animals generated tension, it was much harder to be part of this strange prison and if this were a zoo, I would spend the rest of my life just smiling and feeding until I died. I would grow old eating delicious, without worrying and with an enviable health, like living a century ... but locked up.

I wouldn't even have a woman to accompany me, hugging me and taking care of me, with no opportunity to procreate a beautiful and warm family like my parents did.

- How ironic! - I would be the first man to step on Jupiter, and I am surely already listed in the statistics of the deaths of a failed mission, such as that of the Challenger, which disintegrated a minute and thirteen seconds after the launch, on January 28, 1986 with seven crew.

Yes, I could not stop thinking about Camila, the most important woman in my life, rather, the only one, maybe I was never the same for her, but at least she and my family were the motivation to try not to spend here the rest of my days My goal was to return to the triumphant town for having made history and recover Camila as it would. In this sad room I just wanted to hug her.

We met in childhood in kindergarten and we separated at the university to go to different countries, it was when I started my career at NASA. At seventeen we were dating for two years; it was the first time for both. I was proud to know that I had been the first man in her life, she not only represented that, but also the woman with whom I connected mentally and emotionally. Possibly because my parents divorced at sixteen, causing me deep pain for not being able to share special moments with them. I think that the trauma made me believe in true love, that of a lifetime, which can overcome any misfortune, she meant that to me. Sitting and desolate on the bed passed all those thoughts.

That morning, I guess at the end of February, changed my life. It was a brief moment; as I blink I went from depression to a state of surprise, when for the first time I saw in the room something as amazing as the window, which slowly changed its color to transform into the appearance of an automatic sliding door that opened and in which, slowly, was levitating a body that approached my side.

Immediately another bed was deployed that covered the head, back, hip, feet, until the body was fully lying on it. I approached in a hurry and astonishment, I could barely see the face, I was scrambled by the long, wavy and grotesquely careless hair full of fat. His figure was barely visible by the skins that covered it and the oil smeared on the skin, the smell was unbearable. Even so, I was shortening distance until my right hand was a few inches away from removing the hair from the body, when his left hand took me hard and frightened me. He looked into my eyes in a terrifying way and threw a huge bite to my right arm, from which he held on until I pulled away, fortunately the bite was not so deep, because I managed to get away quickly, while involuntarily, by an act reflex, with the lower palm of my hand, I hit his chin very hard and fell back unconscious.

While a lot of blood was draining, I felt desperate to have no way to relieve the pain and stop the bleeding, I was shocked thinking that I could die there by a simple bite without the necessary care. The pain was terrible, I lay on the bed and just at the height of the bite, two round-shaped objects held my arm while a very thin needle that I barely felt entered my vein. I began to feel very sleepy.

Day 5. An uncomfortable guest.

I woke up and jumped in fear when I saw again next to my bed that human specimen that had been introduced to my cell, room, or whatever it might be called, and that had mortally wounded me. However, when he turned to see my injured arm, he was perfectly healed.

However, I was scared to have a few meters away from the unknown attacker, surprised by the healing that had been done to me, but especially astonished to discover the sculptural body of my companion, without clothes and clean.

- It was a woman! -Her body was perfect, not like that of an excessively thin model, or feminine like a lady, but strong like Camila's, with big legs thicker than mine, a broad back without being masculine. An ostentatious and lush chest. It showed the thick complexion, like that of a Saxon with dark complexion, it was noted that she was doing an intense work under the sun, because the dark of her skin seemed to be due to the effect of exposure to sunlight.- Where could it be? Who else sent space missions to Jupiter? The Russians? - China didn't seem, it didn't have slanted eyes. She woke up and I was trembling with fear at not knowing what would happen, how she would react, maybe she was a mentally ill person, or she would have stayed that way after her expedition failed. I was impressed by the turquoise blue of her gaze, which complicated to define its origin. We stared at each other and before she attacked me again, I tried to find out more.

— Hi - I said as my voice cracked in fear. - I am Robert Anstead crew of the Pioneer 17, who had a mishap a couple of days ago - she with her lost look did not listen to me. - what's your name? Speak English?

Her eyes were intimidated, my fear returned, she only emitted strange grunts, however, I tried to be alerted all the time to any movement to prevent another aggression. Being a scientist always makes you think about theories, so I started to formulate some about their presence.

Theory one: she had also drifted in some space mission that could have happened recently or many years ago and because of that she could not express herself well, because she lived in captivity like this, she was in a wild state. Was she born in that environment, so she was unable to articulate words?

Theory two: there were human beings on some other planet, it could be far-fetched but logical, but where did that specimen come from? In theory, the superior civilization that had us locked up in a probable space zoo had to place the same species in the same place, for this reason she was with me, even though her world was millions of kilometers away. It sounded absurd, but for someone who was used to seeing any kind of surprising situations thanks to science, it was a possibility.

That of the species I deduced because moments before I entered the room, when I approached the door and after peering through the window I managed to look at the sides of the room where we were and in a barely noticeable way I saw other similar rooms with some beings that barely appreciated each other, but with a physiognomy totally different from that of humans. Which confirmed one of my theories, I was an animal on display in a space zoo.

My anguish was increasing; coupled with the despair of spending the rest of my days locked up, now, knowing that I would do it with someone trying to attack me all the time, my life was in danger.

That day I tried my best to try to communicate with her with signs and gestures, we had to agree to coexist and I didn't see how to achieve it. But I had to try, and I started with the simplest and most

importantly, show her that she should not attack me, that we were both prisoners. In a day I could not teach her what any human being learns in decades, however, I advanced a lot, I managed to make her see that we were the same species and that I did not seek to hurt her, however, when trying to touch her hand to shake it in peace , she continued to show aggressiveness, without hurting me.

I know that anyone would not sleep with the stress of having a possible aggressor beside them, a potential murderer, but that day I felt too weak, my body needed to rest and my eyes began to close automatically, so I had no choice but to trust her and rest a little on the bed that was a delight, after all, what would be the difference if she killed me that night or lived bored between those four walls many more years, it didn't matter.

Day 6. The coexistence.

I was desperate not being able to communicate verbally with her, although I chose to think that her original language was one that I did not know, it was only to deal with signs and gestures. It helped me a lot what happened daily to build the learning, such as food, which I requested with gestures and touching the imperceptible board on the wall. It reminded me of Iván Pavlov's studies on operant conditioning with dogs, which I could salivate when I heard the bell announcing mealtime, so I used that logic to try to program it and survive in that place.

I did not understand how a strong and beautiful woman had come out of a bad and smelly body overnight, apparently when she slept many things happened that I did not understand, for example, those responsible - let's call them that - from this place that combined species, they had made Sea presentable, that's what I called her because her hair was like the ocean; when I saw her for the first time, fluttering and frightening as in a storm, but after polishing her, it seemed exciting, it was always my fantasy to hold behind the wavy hair of a lady.

I think that the best thing of that day was to change my depression for hope, to feel alone and abandoned for the rest of my days, at least I could have a partner while we were alive. This is life, then we see how catastrophes are joy, as I could smile again, teaching a girl to behave and act. At least I went from a hopeless and terrifying future to a more encouraging one.

I was never a talkative person, mine was always to be locked in my computer, studying to achieve my place in history. However, I necessarily worked as a professor, to give back to the country my education.

I knew that the best way to learn something was to practice it, so I kept talking about telling my whole life so that she would become familiar, and through words, teach her my language.

– Beautiful Sea - I don't know if women really have that sixth sense, but when I mentioned those simple two words their countenance changed, as if I realized the meaning of what my lips were trying to express and I smile.- You understand me? You, Sea, are very beautiful. -and I stole another smile, the second since she appeared in my room.

It was also complicated to be looking at her naked all the time. I did wear the last layer of my flight uniform, thus saving me the embarrassment of noticing the erections it caused me. I didn't have many options to entertain ourselves, so I started thinking about what we could do just with our bodies. Perhaps it was not the most advisable for a relationship of partners, but it was the first thing that occurred to me, to teach it to play defeated.

At first it was hard for her to understand that I was not going to hurt her, when she understood I discovered that her strength was too much and, on several occasions, she defeated me.

Unintentionally I brushed her chest with my arm sometimes and that caused me immense excitement, it melted me to feel the softness of her breasts, but when I touched her legs and unintentionally touched near her groin, I was about to ejaculate, after so much time without a partner, my body blushed at the slightest stimulation and more if that stimulus was a beautiful and strange woman.

I could add to my great achievements having taught Sea how to smile, every time she beat me playing, I kept doing it. The waste of energy caused me fatigue, there came a time when she wanted to continue playing, like a child who cannot stop or run out.

I just lay down on my bed and inhaled deeply several times while the dream beat me.

Day 7. Party.

Already for the seventh day, I knew a lot about the operation of the home where we lived, I decided to call it that to reduce the anxiety of confinement. That day dawned brighter than the previous two, it reminded me of my summer vacation on the beaches of Veracruz, in Mexico, with my mother's family: the waves shining with the sunlight shaking my body, I remembered the breeze and my tongue longed for the bitter and icy taste of the craft beer that is prepared there. If the Veracruz people have magic for something, it is to make art, and they always did it, it was a type of beer that I had never tried.

Extreme was my surprise when I lowered the deck where my food was served, there was a glass container with the golden label engraved with the name of Veracruz; the beer was delicious and sparkling, at a perfect temperature, ice cold.

That was not the only surprising thing, coincidentally, but with less intensity, I also craved the salt bud, that Veracruz-style delicacy prepared on the grill with various spices.

Maybe this part of the story does not help to believe in my words; I also know that whoever reads me will think the same as me, that this place could provide us with everything we needed to live in the best way as we aged.

I began to analyze that this is precisely what is done in zoos, try to reproduce as much as possible the habitat of each species, provide them with a place similar to their home and feed them with what they are used to, here the different thing was that in the first place Humans are a species that has reason and does not act by instinct, so they are more difficult to satisfy, no other would have wanted grilled fish.

Second, the most admirable were those details, the cold beer just as my papillae would have wished, the fresh food, definitely who was the owner of this space zoo, must be from a much more developed civilization to ours, which on the one hand it made me feel safe that they would not harm us, but it still distressed me, because if so, an escape was impossible.

I toasted my can of beer with her glass of water and said - Cheers, beautiful Sea - and even took a sip to try my drink, she made a grim gesture for her bitterness.

— Sea, beautiful- it sounded amazing to hear those words from her lips, especially because I knew what they meant, since I didn't say it by naming something but as if wondering if I still thought it was.

— Yes - I said while I nodded to reinforce the language and to reaffirm what was said - you are beautiful Sea - pointing it with the index finger.

That day the cold room made her shiver. I noticed it because her brown, tanned and imposing body bristled. I put my hand on her shoulder trying to touch her skin and then hug her so she wouldn't feel the ravages of the cold so much. She spotted and accidentally hit my nose with a slight scratch, we turned to see each other while I tried to show her that she was doing it for her good.

— Calm down, Sea, when the skin comes into contact, the cold decreases - I said as I touched my hand a little with her.

— Skin - it seems that he understood the meaning of that word, was the only thing she managed to pronounce.

And so little by little she allowed my body to cover it and feeling better, I don't know what it would have felt, but I immediately reacted, my body played tricks on me, it was something involuntary. It was just when I hugged her tighter and my skin covered almost all of hers. She was tall and my member was just below her pelvis.

I expected an equally aggressive reaction to the previous ones, but inexplicably it didn't happen, she stayed still in my arms for several minutes. The strangest thing is that when I turned to see her, I didn't make any gesture, any other man would have thought that I enjoyed the involuntary reaction of my member. But I, who had been with her for a couple of days, after experiencing the strangest situations, knew that if she didn't react negatively, it wasn't because she wanted me to be close to her private parts. Rather the reaction was of innocence, that she did not interpret any malice in that movement, I fantasized to think that in her life she had not only not had a man nearby but had not even seen a male organ.

By her reactions I could almost be sure, that seemed very difficult to believe.

- What if she came from another planet where there were also human beings? - It would be news that would create science, and not only that, it would be a theory that would modify and help to understand many situations about our survival.

With a planet Earth about to collapse, with extreme temperatures due to climate change that generated therefore neglect, deforestation, the excessive use of minerals, metals, gas, oxygen, oil, left few alternatives to continue inhabiting it.

Sea could be the key to finding another place where the ideal conditions for living existed, perhaps the first fruit I tried came from that place, I imagined tasting it, along with thousands of new and delicious fruits in another nature, far from contamination. Yes, I was speculating to lose my excitement, is that it was not only her skin that excited me, her rarity and her inexplicable behavior also caused me a great desire psychologically. As I could understand, I expressed that we could even sleep in each other's arms to reduce the cold that I could feel during the night.

I lay on her bed and hugged her, the reaction was the same, so I decided to relax and try to rest a little, I felt very excited to feel her in my arms, and for the first time I wanted to make love to her.

Day 8. At dawn.

I woke up, I think, at dawn, according to my biological clock. And yes, I was still hugging her while she slept, and yes, the erection had not waned, I would not know if it was all night or just a few moments before waking up, but there it was.

Her neck was stylized, -my imagination began to fly. - As a man of science, I decided to try to solve the problem in a simple way, to find that my body would reach an excitement so that the fluids would leave unstoppable without the minimum friction.

I tried, but I couldn't. Then I speculated on what would happen if she and I were together, I even thought about taking that risk, I lost nothing and even more if I would spend the rest of my life here. Although I was morally restrained, because doing so would be like taking it by force, however, she was very strong, equal or more than me, so without problems I would move away.

I was in that ethical debate when a third variable emerged, the bluntest, the one that made me an unscrupulous being - What would happen if another human being were recruited to live in the same cell? - I was jealous to imagine Sea with another. I had grown fond of her in a couple of days. At first, I thought it was because of loneliness, but then I realized that, in any continent and context, Sea was an extraordinary and different woman. And it would probably be the last one I saw in my life, and I made the decision.

Her back attached to mine made me deliberate that the simplest thing would be to penetrate her like this, in the end that my member was only a few inches away from her intimacy, something that she didn't even care about, she would almost swear was innocence.

I started kissing her neck, she turned and we were facing each other, I tried to brush her lips, but she made a confused face, although she followed me. When I noticed that there was no discomfort I put her on her back and placed myself on top of her, at first she tried to push me off, but I calmed her down by kissing her and gently taking her by the arms, I was nowhere to enter and I didn't know what her reaction would be, Especially if she was a virgin. That's why I thought about it so much while kissing her neck and that tingling made her move abruptly ecstatic, I loved seeing her like this, especially feeling her. We were kissing for several minutes, but my whole body was shaking when I did not know what her reaction would be when I took her, I was not an expert, it is more the only woman I had been with was Camila, my first and only love, and from there I was lost on to her being. The same could happen here without taking any risk because I was the only man by her side.

I could not penetrate her slowly since, if she did not like or hurt, she would rule out trying again, it would be the same as tearing a splinter out of a lion's claw, the pain could wake up a lethal weapon, it must be very fast and contain the attack already out of pain, pleasure or anger. I inhaled deeply to inflate my lungs to the top feeling like every effort filled my chest and stood with a great strength, I closed my eyes accommodating where they started their lips that were a little damp after my kisses and caresses, and with force I entered her.

Her scream was deafening because her mouth was right next to my right ear, at the same time I also screamed because I felt a lot of pain since it was dry inside.

I felt like my skin was torn a little, but I was still excited and began to make the move out and in while she tried to dodge it, I put my arms under her to hug her tight and I couldn't let go, until a couple of minutes then, because of the great excitement, I finished, while looking at my side her strong and turned legs.

It was an intense battle that did not last long, holding her arms trying to get rid of me was an odyssey and I ended up exhausted, I didn't know how she would react after this, so I immediately got up and sat on my bed while watching her reaction taking distance. I was totally stunned, she didn't understand what had happened, while watching my semen drain from her outer lips.

With signs I tried to explain that it was nothing bad, she was also tired and was more frightened to see her intimate parts bleed, so I took off my shirt to clean it and show her that I just wanted to help. So, she understood and calmed down when the blood disappeared. She lay down and fell asleep, I would have given anything to know what was going through her mind.

I could not sleep, I assumed there were a few moments before dawn; my gaze was lost on the whitish ceiling of the room, remembering every sublime moment. With the adrenaline rush that did not let me sleep, I would take the opportunity to know how it was that the window began to open in the morning and calculate the time depending on the intensity of the sun's rays.

Besides, it was an enigma that normally at night, while I was sleeping, things happened that I did not understand the next day, such as the healing of my arm or the cleaning of Sea. That was how I discovered surprising things: the window began to open as each ray of sun crashed into it, so the first one saw clearly how it went through a small hole. And so, each ray was a shot of light that crossed the white wall, gradually illuminating the interior of the room until it was fully illuminated.

I took the opportunity to look out and observe what the species locked up in the other rooms did, of course, most of them slept, the difference with the previous day is that the cell on my left side was occupied, a day before it remained empty, but a creature that barely was able to distinguish himself by his small size and he lived there.

When Sea woke up, I brought her food to the bed and thus be condescending. Also with the appearance of my favorite beer a day before I had discovered that the system we were in would provide us with whatever it was if we wanted to, so I invoked some objects to write and color and have a more didactic way of teaching our language .

Crayons and a notebook with large sheets for drawing appeared on a tray that was displayed on the right side of the bed.

I took the opportunity to show her what my planet was like, she seemed to be unaware of the places I drew, such as the Eiffel Tower with which I even gave her a kiss, since it was a symbol of romanticism, the Statue of Liberty, the Pyramids of Egypt, the Taj Mahal, the Pyramids of Teotihuacán, the fascinating Grand Canyon where I imagined traveling with her, Big Ben in London, Niagara Falls and also the Iguazu Falls in South America.

Finally she fell asleep trying to draw, the truth was not something recognizable, so I took the notebook and put it on the floor between both beds to get ready to sleep, it had been an unforgettable day and I wished it was for her too, although I didn't say it or demonstrated, even so, before going to sleep I wrote down the probable date of that moment, adding that it was day eight, in case my calculations failed.

Day 9. Revealing images.

What better way to wake up than with Sea next to me serving breakfast, corresponding to the nice detail of the previous day. The effusive hug she gave me made me feel that I knew how important our first meeting had been for both of us. In a few days and in an unknown place, I went from calvary to fullness.

While having breakfast with a big appetite, she took the notebook and continued coloring. Soon the brown figures were assembling recognizable shapes and resembling something that my mind gave no credit. - They looked like prehistoric animals! - and my theory that she was a human being from another planet was proven.

Although I must admit that I was horrified to think that such animals lived on their planet and that the drawings looked like works of art, it really showed talent.

After several days I found an item vending machine in front of the bed, I just had to put my hands on the wall, want something and it automatically appeared. I guess our captor read the mind, but how far could he satisfy our requests? Would there be any limits?

I did a test: I put my left hand on the wall wishing a steaming cup of Veracruz coffee, like the one my grandmother made for me when I visited it during the summer of the Gulf of Mexico. And so, it was the most delicious aromatic infusion appeared served in some metal cups, material that allowed to keep the drink warm, like that of double steel that we humans use to achieve the same effect.

As I drank sitting on the corner of my bed, I watched her paint, like this, naked, with her impressive hips and dark skin; Tanned, we know that painters are eccentric, but I have not heard of anyone who works without clothes. Obviously, Sea was not Camila, nor did she resemble her, however, I assume that I became fond of her in no time; what took years to spend with Camila, with everything and her great beauty, intelligence and elegance. Sea didn't need any tricks or makeup to make me happy.

On the other hand, I was worried that she only drew animals, so I developed three theories.

- The first, who had not understood what I was asking you to show me, which usually happens, especially when we talk with a person who speaks a different language. Maybe she understood that I wanted something related to the place where we were in captivity and that's why she drew those animals from past eras.

- The second was that on this planet there were such species that disappeared on earth, which was quite strange because they were supposed to be a civilization developed enough to live with such ancient animals, or managed to keep them based on scientific discoveries, safe or even cloned as in the famous science fiction film "Jurassic Park."

- The third seemed inconceivable because there were several details tormenting me. For example, the animal skins that covered her when she first entered the room, without any craft work on her clothes; the smell of oil poured on your skin, probably smeared to prevent the cold on your planet; the inability to express themselves verbally, being that it comes from a more advanced civilization; the physical: the hips and thick legs, unusual in a human; the aggressiveness with unknown people and the hair, although lush like a beautiful ficus tree, it looked careless.

My conclusions pointed out that Sea had been at that time, along with these animals, thousands of years ago. Sounds bold, however, the evidence made me formulate the illogical theory. But how could a prehistoric human species be here, in the same cell of a space zoo?

During my studies at NASA I learned incredible things, but these days most of my paradigms had collapsed. Since my arrival I had already been surprised to have seen species that I never imagined and now this ... For a moment, I had the feeling of being immersed in a dream.

Tired and confused, I decided to lie on her thighs again while I talked to her about my ideas; she didn't understand, but I felt relieved. I tried not to think anymore, in the end what did it matter if it was true, at that time I was very happy and that was the important thing.

Day 10. New animal.

A noise interrupted my dream. It was done by a being that I imagine was close to our cell, it was not strong like the roar of a lion or like the cock of a rooster, rather little tolerable, like the buzz that remains after an explosion. So, at first, I thought it was a machine and it would stop soon, but it took almost an hour. However, she slept deeply, did not flinch.

Since Sea had arrived, the awakening had become great: the first thing my eyes saw at dawn was her naked, sublime body, lying next to me; that morning she slept on her back, displaying the big nipples on her chest.

It had been an hour of that unpleasant sound and she did not made a minimum movement, so I took the moment to try to penetrate her. Thus, I was entering slightly, avoiding waking her and it seemed that she enjoyed it, even if it was in dreams, because she did not wake up and an involuntary smile was drawn on her face.

She opened her eyes when she was about to finish, and it didn't take long to do so because her body, just seeing her, excited me too much. She was frightened and with excessive force threw me to the side of her bed, fortunately before she pushed me, I managed to ejaculate.

I was between pleasure and laughter when I saw her sleepy. Then, she smiled wickedly as she realized what I was doing before she woke up; She immediately hugged me tenderly. With the gesture I felt that I knew the power of her body over me; and how indispensable her company was becoming.

– A few days ago, you were not here, and today I think I could not be without your presence. - I told.

Sea seemed to understand my words, because a tear ran down her face and hugged me harder, making me feel how important it was. She pronounced "Sea" ... and then drew us in the notebook.

I asked what it was, but she interrupted my comment by putting one of her fingers on my lips, telling me to wait.

It seemed that we were in a cave, the plants were huge, but of different colors. I assumed that was her home and I was flattered to see us together. At that moment, after trying and teaching her how to communicate, I felt her protector, that man capable of satisfying her; I don't know if all the men have experienced it, but it even made me forget the failure of the mission to Jupiter.

I touched the wall of desires, a name I hypothetically assigned to always please me, and I imagined a music player, to teach her to dance close to my arms. Fortunately, a very sophisticated one appeared, and I immediately looked for some ideal melody to start my classes, it must be a ballad, that genre that was almost eradicated in 2027, displaced reggaeton and hip hop.

I thought of a classic and to my mind came a Latin music, that ballad style with a little rhythm called bachata, the chosen one was the Dominican Juan Luis Guerra with a song that shook me when my father took my mother's waist ... now I realize what happened when after dancing, they sent me to sleep.

"I will live in your memory, like a simple downpour of stars and sprites, I will roam your belly ..."

"You will live in my dreams as indelible ink ..."

The first notes sounded, I stood up, took her waist gently and began to wiggle her slowly to the rhythm of the song, she smiled and radiated joy.

"I stayed in your pupils my good, I no longer close my eyes, I threw myself deep and drowned in the seas of your departure, your departure ..."

The afternoon fell and the moon appeared creating a romantic atmosphere; I whispered the plans I had to make in the cell every day.

Feeling lost on four walls, his arrival inspired me to organize activities and live them with her. We danced many songs until we fell in bed and just hugged each other all night.

Day 11. Immense joy.

I got up motivated, it was one of those days in which since you see the ray of light you begin to thank God for being alive, for being happy, just when I felt that I had lost all hope. Despite the confinement, I was grateful for the aroma of coffee, which I am sure was from Veracruz for the unique taste; for being healthy to enjoy the delicacies received at each meal; for every drop of water for my body and how I could access it without any setback, until I felt it run down the throat and body.

Especially, I felt gratified for having found what was most likely love, I didn't care about the name, I was just happy, period. And I thanked again for the strange woman who had entered my life and had become a balm to continue and overcome any depression. Without imagining it, I had found in fearful uncertainty what I always looked for in an ordinary way, and it suddenly appeared so extraordinarily. I didn't need anything else.

Knowing that I had enough tools to be able to teach my language, I started classes by writing the most important words in the notebook, before beginning to show grammar and syntax. Sea showed great intelligence and quickly memorized the words, the difficult thing was that when she pronounced them, she could not even emit any sound, it was noted that her speech was not very developed, until I came to think that it was a health problem.

Two days flew by, trying affectionately; for moments we alternated the lessons with romantic meals that I chose and that fortunately she liked and with a little kiss in each attempt to pronounce the words.

Obviously, I couldn't stop possessing her, her naked body excited me, we did it up to six times a day. The only thing I could achieve in my forty-eight hours of intense work as a language teacher, was

That she pronounced my name, which caused me an emotion like when a son says dad for the first time.

– Robert-

– Yes, beautiful Sea, Robert, that's my name.

She smiled when she saw the joy that caused me to hear that word from her lips. I hugged her and kissed her, at first, she barely moved her lips, but after a few days, she let herself be carried away by every subtle movement of my tongue and each interaction became more pleasant, so much that I didn't need to kiss her for so long to get excited and possess her. Although I felt a very strong discomfort in the knees, beaten by playing soccer since childhood, seeing her hips widen as she pressed against the white floor, made up for everything. I finished and was soaked after experiencing pleasure and pain at the same time. I lay in bed, ecstatic, without strength and with my knees marked, flushed and hurt.

Day 13. My family.

I felt that my veins were about to explode when they tried to remove my three-year-old little girl, Sea and the little man from the house, Rob. It was as if parts of my body were ripped off ... everything was happening in slow motion ... just as once his mother had entered, now they took my children without me being able to do something.

I woke up drenched in sweat, my body was shaking from head to toe, I looked towards the ceiling, I took a deep breath feeling as each volume of oxygen passed through my lungs until I inflated them to the top and regained my breath, I sat on the bed and burst into tears.

I had mixed feelings: I cried with happiness because it was just a bad dream, but also of depression, which beset my mind from the nightmare.

What would become of me and a probable family in this place, locked up? I would never have wanted something like that for my children, I was immensely happy with Sea anywhere, but they, the children, how could they play and develop their skills in a habitat like this. Would they change cells? Would you allow them to be free? Where would they live if they were free? On the planet of Sea or mine? Would they develop the same love for their parents as I do with mine, by being in captivity? What behaviors would a human being develop in this way?

The questions caused me a headache, so at breakfast there appeared a tablet like aspirin, which I ingested and lay down while Sea painted a colorful landscape. When I woke up, she approached and with signs I understood that the drawing was dedicated to me. Suddenly I felt a knot in my stomach.

Despite enjoying the moment, I kept feeling afraid that it was all a dream, which I would wake up at any time lying in the hammock of my parents' ranch in Mission, Texas.

The routine began to invade us, but it was not bad, there are times that the routine can also fall in love and become the reason for existing. Every day it was to get up, see her gaze, her extraordinary body, make love to her, make coffee and watch her paint ... she and her drawings were two works of art together.

Instead of getting bored, every day I liked it better, I could live like that forever.

Obviously, I was beset by uncertainty for not knowing who or who had us held and for what. Were we living in a zoo ?, were we ornament and learning from other species who visited us to know human nature ?, would we be part of the food chain of the inhabitants of this strange planet ?, or did we belong to an investigation in which did they keep us watching day and night to determine how we behave and how our body works, something more sophisticated than opening aliens, as we did on Earth? And the worst question was, when would the day be? in case of being planned for the dinner of a superior being. Then I thought: if we were going to be someone else's food or energy they would not treat us well, we would not have all the luxury that we enjoyed in the confinement, I would not drink coffee after making love every morning.

However, I remembered that in some places they raise cattle and even music they put on cows so as not to stress them and achieve better quality meat. That is why I woke up every day thinking that I was probably the last, so I lived it to the fullest and happily at his side.

Day 14. Contact.

I opened my eyes determined to discover the truth no matter how painful it was. Let's see … this species was supposed to read my mind, but the answer to my questions that were generated could be subjective, an invention of my neurons was not sure that it was the answer of a higher being or beings. I needed something tangible and concrete. I took another sip of the delicious morning coffee and thought about the options to achieve the goal … - how about trying to touch the wall asking for the answers! - or writing the questions on the sheets of paper where Sea made her works of art …I started simply, write a question on a sheet, chose a fairly visible color, magenta and added a little black to make the letters bigger, and even, so that it could be seen from any camera, which were surely installed in the room.- "Who you are?"-I left it on Sea's bed waiting for an answer. They spent several minutes even hours while watching Sea paint and at every moment I looked at the paper with the written question. Then I sat and ate the dried meat eggs prepared for us that morning. And I could not miss toast with butter, although I was rationing the amounts I imagine because of the large number of calories, but at least I could enjoy a piece smeared with strawberry jam. Having no response, after a couple of hours, I continued with the agenda of the day: teach language to Sea.

At first, she learned very slowly, but every day that passed showed an ascending intelligence; Sometimes I was surprised how she handled all the resources at our disposal in the room.

Unlike me, her food was always very simple, no elaborate stews, almost every day I ate grilled fish, without condiments. However, she also enjoyed as much as I did the onion octopus that I ordered, which was delicious, very similar to what they prepare on the coast of the Gulf of Mexico. This day I also noticed a zero influx of visitors to what I called "the universal zoo" in which I was. It could

be the day of rest and as there were no creatures watching us, through the window I tried to see beyond the small forum in front of me. The landscape looked full of lush vegetation, including trees that stood out for their height, like the giant sequoia trees in California. With the forum empty, I decided to touch the wall of desires and asked that the forum levels disappear to better observe the landscape behind. Thus, each link of the auditorium retreated until it disappeared.

I was perplexed by the exotic colors of flowers and plants. There were reddish fruits with a cylindrical shape, completely smooth, wet with drops apparently of rain. My mouth was watering, I wanted to taste the fruits that most likely were not even edible. - What would happen if I asked for it on the wall of wishes? - If it appears on the food tray, it would be an indication that they were edible.

I couldn't wait, so I did it and once again I was granted, I was ready to try the delicacy.

It was about noon and I felt a little sleepy, I had slept little because of the uncertainty of the place; I took the fruit in my hands and bit it without restraint. Its flavor was indescribable, perhaps a little of the sweetness of the mango with the texture of a fresh peach and the acidity resembled that of blackberries. The temperature was perfect: cold and wet. I offered Sea a little, and she ate from my hand, so, figuratively, I always wanted to have her; eating from my hand, near me.

In less than an hour I began to feel different, very strongly, like when you take any medication for circulation, I had a lot of energy. I assumed that the same thing happened to Sea, because of slowly painting with stealth, her strokes were faster and more accurate. The displacement she made around her painting was also lighter and her hips had a cadence that excited me in an unprecedented way. I went from sleepy to lively, like when you drink a cup of coffee. I walked

around the room in search of new alternatives, meditating on all the questions raised above and tormenting my mind. I walked quickly, I had time not to feel so vigorous. I watched Sea's work of art from all angles ... and her hips.

For moments, she looked at me sideways and her pupils seemed dilated, I presumed that the agitation was because she also wanted to be with me. The last deep and lascivious look she had when drawing a woman's hair on the canvas, probably hers, activated my animal instinct and I started biting her lips in a strong and passionate way, she corresponded to the degree of cutting my lip a little lower. Later, I gently bit her neck, but I already wanted, since the glaring glances potentiated by the unknown fruit emerged, reaching her legs, they bewitched me, they were a sign of strength, her golden color, like that of the coffee beans roasted by the sun and her muscles drove me crazy. I savored them in a thousand ways: soft, slow, strong, in all positions, until I approached her groin, causing her breathing to accelerate and make sounds of pleasure. When I penetrated her, I felt with the strength of an oak, also confident of the aphrodisiac of the strange fruit, with all the strength of my legs penetrating it, I thought at that moment to have control, but it was an illusion, because I was the slave of the movement and texture of her legs, I became submissive between them, and my energy weakened until it was over.

I was there ... lying ... ecstatic and frustrated that I couldn't do more for her. If the elixir had given me a lot of energy, for Sea it had been double, I was whole, as if nothing had happened. She got up, served me coffee and kept painting serene, but making strokes faster and more perfect.

The moral was good, I decided that the fruit would only prove it, it was a very powerful weapon to give it to her, I could not control it.

Day 15. The revelation.

- "You know who I am, I don't think you doubt my existence" - The letters were large, blue and formed on the wall where the window was. I turned to Sea's bed, I was sitting, making no noise seeing the letters. With the limitations of communication between us, I understood that I was questioning about the message that appeared that morning.

I explained that it was something unimportant, since I didn't understand the answer either. Then, I analyzed the question to ask. I took a sheet of paper and a color.

- "Why do you have us in captivity?" - The previous response slowly faded, from left to right. We both looked curiously at the wall waiting for the next one; out of despair, a nervous tic was activated in my right leg; Sea realized and to calm me down she served me some coffee, we sat on the same bed, drank and waited, but every second was lacerating.- "You are not in captivity, you are free to go wherever you want" - The lyrics began to disappear again, I hurried to write the next question. I jumped from the bed of fright when I discovered aberrant creatures near the wall. The window was open and apparently the show should continue, the zoo was in operation. I kept the question in mind and the most intense colored pencil about to write it on paper.

I went back to bed, sat down and meditated on the possible identity of our prisoner; I was afraid to be in the hands of someone who wanted to harm us, or by aliens of an intellectual level greater than the human being, being the target of his observation; there was also the possibility that this had been caused by the accident of the ship, perhaps I had been exposed to some chemical compound and was delirious.

It was time for lunch, and I decided to order my favorite food, as everything was so confusing, I no longer knew if the wall was real, if the food existed or was similar, with a very similar taste. But what else did I do if he was happy with Sea!

Galician octopus for both. I gave her snacks, at first, she made a gesture of distaste, but when he tasted the seafood seasoned with spices and a little oil, the countenance changed, and she liked it. I told her through signs and words how fascinating her works were, that I liked to see her painting and, above all, that I loved every stroke of the various colors expressed on the paper; I was not a connoisseur in the field, but I recognized an unequaled style, especially because of the way of doing it, naked. A majestic work of art creating another work of art.

We had a pleasant afternoon, fortunately we had become accustomed to living in a showcase where they could observe our lives, she never showed fear in the situation, she was braver than me. It was complicated to eat in front of a multitude of strange beings and apart grotesque. Even sometimes I gave up doing it because of that unpleasant feeling. Already relaxed, after eating, hugging, my frustrated question came to my mind. - "If we are free, why can't we get out of here and live outside these four walls?"

Suddenly, in one of the corners of the room, the furthest from our beds, a tray with objects that could not distinguish due to the distance was deployed, so we both got up to look at them closely. We approached slowly and when we had them at hand, my body shuddered, that moment was a frank affront.

Sea did not understand what was happening, but I could feel my face disheveled, the product of confusion. I touched the objects to determine if they were real, imaginary or a hologram. I realized that they did exist and threw them back into the tray. I pulled Sea towards the bed, I couldn't understand how the ship's manual controls had arrived there, the plaque with my full name, the position as commander in chief of the Pioneer 17 and my date of birth.

I decided to keep the idea that they were replicas, I was afraid to activate the commands with the voice code and discover more surprising things, such as that the room could be the ship, or that at that time I could be free and return to Earth. - Was that a possible answer to my question? We were both free to leave at the desired time? - But I would not leave Sea, that was the big question, - what would happen if I returned to Earth? Would Sea also go with me?

Day 16. Poetry.

Theories and more theories came to my mind, maybe it was there because Sea and I wanted it that way. That day I did not order an espresso coffee in the morning but a black tea, I wanted to forget about the issue of my ship controls, but it came to my mind every moment, there was no better way to forget everything than watching Sea painting, although this time she turned the sheet of paper beckoning me to not observe her work, making me understand that it was a surprise which made me quite happy. The surprise that came from her would be something beautiful and different in those moments. Even so, watching her paint, now straight on, was still the most beautiful thing for me.

I was even more excited by watching her focused gaze, her smile enjoying every stroke, her lush body moving, and her hair covering her cheeks. She stared at me several times, I could almost bet she was painting something about me, every time I threw a kiss and she smiled, so it was several times until I didn't hold back and signaled her to approach me pretending that I needed something from her, and what a need. When that imposing body of overwhelming thighs stood in front of me, I was sitting helpless in the face of such temptation and with its most intimate part a few inches away, I hugged her body pressing my right cheek to her pubis and my hands surrounding her hips. She corresponded by putting her arms on my head and began to kiss me, I pulled with her hands her buttocks towards me so that she fell sitting in front of my legs while she continued kissing me.

Her body lost in my face like seawater stirred by the wind excited me too much and more on that occasion making sounds before not heard by me. She moved very slowly, and I just placed my hands behind my bed while she pressed her chest to my face, and her movements made me finish.

She got up to continue her work of art, while I lay in bed, exhausted and satisfied. I took a sheet of paper and a color and tried to order several words from my soul. I didn't remember writing something like that since I was a child and I was fascinated by poetry. However, this was not a desire to make poetry, but involuntary movements of my hands guided by the deepest part of my being.

In a world without apparent rules I could freely write my feelings towards her, many seemed wild and uncivilized, however, my hands moved not driven by those motivations.

Contrasting words appeared on the paper, my fingers gliding mechanically defining every sensation since I met her. From the most aberrant wild thoughts probably due to my fear of losing her to the purest unleashed by a unique woman I never thought I found and less in captivity.

As if we were synchronized, we finished at the same time, the final point of my verses was the last line of his drawing work.

She rolled her picture and put it to the side of my bed, I decided to do the same ritual for when she gave me that surprise I would correspond with a small detail, I never compared her talent to paint with mine to write. I felt a monkey juggling the insult of our kidnapper, making a soccer ball appear in front of our beds, just when the stage was full of tiny beings of all colors, but apparently of the same species. As we bring students from schools to zoos and amusement parks. Until that moment I had not felt so humiliated, I was never good for the sport, although I was a fan of the Dallas Cowboys, I didn't even know how to throw a ball.- "Damn it" - I wrote on paper and began to consume itself as if it were devoured by fire, but there was no flame was just the effect, which scared me for being out of the ordinary. Apparently, someone had bothered my comment, perhaps folly, but it was offensive to put ourselves as pets.

I asked for a bottle of wine on the wall of wishes with the notion of maybe not getting it because of my written words moments before, however, a bottle of Chilean red wine, Carmenere, my favorite appeared. We toast to have finished our gift for a special occasion, a birthday, a month of having met, Christmas, New Year, whatever date, I just waited for the closest to see the surprise that Sea had drawn for me. The afternoon was falling, and the window began to darken, I adored these moments because we were practically both alone, as in our home.

I sprayed some wine on her chest pretending to do it involuntarily, she believed it because she didn't bother and hugged me when she saw my face feeling guilty, it was an excellent trick to test her skin, but now bathed in wine. And so, I went down the path of that creek passing between her breasts and then reach her belly button and finally kiss the parts that could make her shiver the most. What I did not know until that moment, was that her excitement caused the same in me, but with greater intensity, since it was the first time I kissed the intimate parts of a woman. I was afraid every moment I lived with her because she made me more dependent on her kisses and her body, contrary to what I wanted in each verse of my poetry written for her.

We had a great day, it made me forget all the tribulations, to think only of it, what life on Earth would be like by its side, walking through the fields of Texas, even reaching Mexico without borders, how two different countries could be If your floor was the same.

Day 17. The same dream.

Again, that same dream woke me up minutes before the window was illuminated, it was the worst nightmare, losing your offspring was the most unpleasant thing for anyone and I would not be the exception when Sea and I had a family. I turned left in the background wishing I didn't see those objects that made me so stressed. There they remained a challenge, a great temptation throbbing in my mind every second, drilling every neuron without letting me think. I approached them again and caressed them as I had caressed the land bathed by the Rio Grande, with my fingers I rubbed the plate with my name, although my love for Sea was the most important thing, I missed several things on Earth, my parents.

I wanted to get up and have delicious pancakes served by my mother's secret recipe, or walk the southern roads accompanying my father knowing incredible places like the green paradise of California, or the huge Grand Canyon.

And what about my brothers, the spawned Diego, with his warlike spirit, would probably be a Marine graduate by now. Or my sister, Maria, always laughing with me and supporting me in all my nonsense. Aunt Estela who had been like a second mother to all three. I always wanted a woman, as well as Sea, that no one else could have because she was unique, and now I wanted to share that happiness with my family. I imagined my mother stirring the eggs and butter of the pancakes step by step to teach her how to pamper myself, and my father telling him about our adventures lying in a hammock in California while we were traveling along the southern roads. To Maria arguing with her, feeling the rivalry of sharing my time, to Diego showing her badges or to Aunt Estela with her teachings of the Bible, as she did with me as a child.

I was not very assiduous to accompany her to the Church; however, my faith in God was never weakened, it was always the strongest to face all the challenges, just at that moment I asked myself, where would she be while I am away from my family? Why didn't he allow me to be in my house, with Sea and them together?

There was only one way to know where God was at that time and to prove my faith, I was sure that doing whatever the result would help me to be with Sea, so I pronounced out loud the code data to activate the Ship controls.

"077J18R23A10Y04M16E20E05S13R06A21L"

I was afraid to pronounce the next word, my voice cut off when I finished with the codes, but I looked at Sea lying on her bed and gave me courage.- "Activate" -Now we would see if the Entity or Entities that kept us here were not lying. In the distance in the far corner of me, almost a rectangle of the white wall darkened next to my bed, it was about the size of a door, some noises were heard as when a chain descends an object. I felt that everything was moving, I thought about a tremor, my legs danced on the floor, I looked at Sea and I didn't even move. How could I not feel those intense movements!

– Sea, wake up my love, is shaking- she woke up when she heard my screams, but she didn't believe what was happening, she looked at me terrified and with her little language she told me.-

– Where are you going? –

– Like where I am going baby, nowhere, only that it is shaking - it was when unfortunately, I discovered what she had also done already.

Day 18. What happened?

It wasn't a tremor, it was my body moving involuntarily, sliding my feet on the floor. As attracted by a gravitational force heading to that open door on the side of the room. The door lit and I could see a path of light towards that white hatch that I knew so much, with which I dreamed so many times, was the entrance of the Pioneer 17. I smiled, my happiness was complete, God had heard me, we could be together in the Earth.

When I saw my body moving towards my ship, I felt my chest full of strength, of life to shout at it with the greatest joy.

— Sea, we are leaving my love- I said while drawing an immense smile on my face, it was time to make history, not to reach any planet in the universe first as it should have happened weeks ago, or to write my name in letters of I pray in the book of heroes of the nation, but to tattoo every space in my heart with her name.

I could not stop my journey to the door that led to my ship, I kept smiling at her, gesturing to explain what was happening, waiting anxiously for her to follow my steps, I already wanted to be at home, in my city, at my grandfather's ranch presenting her to all my family and drinking coffee in the morning with my parents and my brothers, I would love those moments and they would surely love it when they met her and saw that she was unique.

Sea was still sitting on the bed watching without moving, which began to irritate me a little, I should be running towards the ship to escape from this place.

— I can't- sentenced with her face that was flooded with tears in an instant. At that moment I felt a stake sticking in my chest, knocking again and again to kill me.

— Are you kidding, Sea? If you and I cannot be separated, come with me, stop frightening me.

— I can't move- and her eyes were crying while her legs were there inexplicably paralyzed. It was when fear began to run through every artery in my body.

— Noooooo, you can't do this to me, Sea- my eyes couldn't see the road even because of the blurryness of my sight blocked by the flow of tears running down my cheeks, I can only beg.

— If you're who I think, you can't do this to me, I beg you.

At that moment another door opened, and I felt relief, I thought that my plea had been heard, at that door I discovered some digital numbers on a board located at the top, it was a label for that entry. When I saw mine, my body froze, sweated and felt every drop of ice on my body, my door also had a number, I could no longer scream or try to run to it, motionless, when I saw it also move involuntarily, sliding, I made the other alternative .-Come on, you can do everything, let me be with her is the only thing I ask- I tried to address that entity without the security of who it was or what happened, but I exhausted my last breath.

It could not be possible, we both moved away to enter at each end of the room to a door with different destinations, but if everything I imagined was true, they were two impossible destinations to join.

We stared at each other without stopping sobbing, that cry that drowns you and eats you inside, that at times you feel your head explode, not only once but forever. I watched her move in slow motion and didn't take her eyes off me either, neither of us blinked, we knew it was probably the last time we would meet. I remembered the lyrics of the song we danced, and it was like putting the last nails on my coffin.

I watched as she took her poetry from the bed and treasured it against her chest, I stretched my right arm as much as I could to take the painting she did for me, as a comfort, there was nothing that could heal me, but at least I would have forever some memory of her. In that last moment I closed my eyes and began to pray no longer for the miracle of taking her with me but because it was fine where she wants me to go and never, no matter how much time passed, she forgot about me.

Back to Pioneer 17, I didn't even need to drive the ship, each of the controls automatically started to activate and the destination was Earth, although there was no way to determine where it was, it was blocked, so, forever.

Day 19. The return.

The journey was so monotonous, I cried every second to remember Sea's arms. Now I was in a real confinement, in a space smaller than that room, and without Sea, I didn't even have the strength to try to take my life and gravity too it made this an almost impossible challenge. I poured some coffee, that container had been there since we were stranded, it was cold, but still it was one of the few things to remember her, that's why I decided to drink it that way. They were the last grains, the rest we had drunk playing chess with John and Joseph Collins. At that moment I looked at the digital board of their vital signs, they appeared as deaths, my soul brothers were gone, I became sadder.

I looked at a touch board next to the controls where John wrote a message on takeoff.

"This trip will change our lives and the vision we have of the world" And what changed, it destroyed us, although in my case there was always the penance of having lived the happiest moments of my life.

Finally, it was time, a couple of days after leaving I took the wrapped painting, as her surprise gift. Seeing each beautiful image, the feeling was contrasting, a pain stronger than the sense until that moment, but also a motivation, a hope, a little joy to see in that green paradise.

In the middle of her world, of her time, between the mountains she was covered with skins similar to those she looked when I met her entering the room, to one side holding her hand as I did most of the time in the room, she had painted myself with finer gestures, I looked younger and more handsome, laughed with tears in the eyes of the tingling caused by her details to capture me, probably she looked at me like that, even bigger and stronger than I was, it was for love.

I thought that the greatest pain I had already experienced, I imagined that my days would be eternally unhappy without her, but if something could make me feel more empty it was the small image that she drew on her left side, beside me. I hated everyone at that time, I launched my fury against who had separated me from her, I felt for a moment that emotion that one dreams of as a child and sees her parents as her greatest heroes, being one day someone was perhaps the most desired goal by any human being. In fractions of a second, observing her painting, I imagined a life beside that being, taking care of him, feeding him, taking him to the field to teach him how to drive or how to play baseball, accompanying me on my road adventures as my father did with me. I wanted to die to discover what would have been the most important news of my life, above stepping on Jupiter and going down in history. Seeing that beautiful baby product of the love of Sea and I, simply ended my desire to live. They were horrible hours of imagining our life as a family in Texas, as a large Latin-style family, that even the dog lived inside at home, with grandparents and uncles. Each kilometer closer to the earth was one further from it, from any possibility because that unknown place did not represent a distance only in space but also in time. Something totally extraordinary.

I was only there for 18 days, unforgettable for me, however, when I arrived on Earth through the back door, without any official reception, only my ship arriving at an abandoned agricultural field, in a place between Mexico and the border with the United States called Colombia, Nuevo León. I opened the hatch of the Pioneer 17 and finally inhaled, my lungs almost burst, it was an incredible sensation to return to Earth, the wind on my cheeks and to be able to breathe the Earth's air. I walked miles until I reached the town, where I realized that it had really been almost a year, it was December 27, 2027, the eve of the new year, 2028.

Today. December 28th.

And this is the story, after hearing my testimony and even believing everything extraordinary in each part of the story, it is quite likely that those who see and hear this will continue to pose the same questions presented by me on my space travel.

Who or who kept us in those days there? I would have no evidence of any specific being; we were just there. - Where in the universe were, we? - It could have been anywhere in space, in any universe. Where were the remains of John and Joseph?

They would not have a grave to go to their anniversaries every year to clue some flowers and perhaps make some hypothetical game of chess on the board of their epitaph. Tell them some anecdotes of the trip and of our lives, even the story of Sea, which hurts me every time I pronounced every letter of her name. - Who could control most of the civilizations and species of the universe, with enough resources to ensure our survival, the technology to determine our optimal conditions, to manage space and time at will? -This was the biggest question. The greatest scientists agree on the theory of a Supreme being, someone had to detonate the Big Bang, even the most scientific atheist believes it. We were probably in the hands of that Supreme being provided with roof, food, oxygen, conditions to perform our homeostasis, and then return in excellent condition, physical at least, to our place of origin.

I could feel fear for that Supreme being, when thinking about his great power, he held us in captivity for a long time, but the only logical thing he could do is to thank us for taking care of ourselves, for protecting us from the species of the outside, for giving us shelter, a pure air to breathe in an unknown atmosphere, and especially for giving me Sea, although briefly, was the most valuable thing in my life.

And although I could feel too much courage against him for suddenly taking away my happiness, I also remembered that whoever agreed to the controls of the Earth and who programmed my return, it was I, a mistake that I will never forgive myself. In the end it was that Supreme being, call his name, who made me meet her, and be happy.

I could continue to torment myself with the experience or rather with the lost, but right now the only thing I will do, even if it is impossible and sounds stupid, will be to look for Sea. It may be impossible to find her, but I have nothing more important in life than life. I hope to see her again, it is better to die trying to capitulate. I will go anywhere for her, I will study day and night to find a way to get to that place, it sounds crazy, but worse would be not to try, at least I knew at the beginning that I had the lost battle, but only to feel the hope of being able to return It made me breathe, to look for that impossible alternative that the religious know as a miracle, was my goal.

I had little evidence of her place of origin, and as a scientist the first step I thought about determining where the earth was where she lived, even calculating the exact year to know where to go. Of her I only had several general data and of her civilization, some drawings in my mind, vague notions, it was like a case to be solved by a detective without any evidence. I began by reviewing the maps of the world through its existence, probably your home was not even a fist of land and would have remained under the sea like most of the ancient territory.

Maybe those verses that I dedicated to her the happiest day of my life help, when we both exchanged our most valuable things, her art and my poetry attempt.

There is probably somewhere evidence that these words were seen, learned or rewritten. Perhaps you can even find some of these verses in an old book copied from a cave painting in a cave.

Probably I can even find some letters of that paper, written in my fist and letter stamped by the weather and the passage of time, in some fossil anywhere in the world, and then begin.